LeAnn Miller

Hooray for Hildy!

Written and Illustrated by:
LeAnn Miller

Dedicated to my best friend, Tonya, who always makes me feel beautiful.

Hildy loved to wear hats.
She had a hat for...

shopping,

5

parties,

playing ball,

and even a hat with a built in fan
to keep her

cool at the beach.

In fact, no one ever saw Hildy without a hat.

Her friends always enjoyed the unique hats - all of them, except Sydney. She made fun of them every chance she got.

One day while shopping at the "Hat Hut",
Hildy and Erika ran into Sydney.
"Nice hat, Hildy!
It's the silliest thing I have ever seen!"

Hildy blushed as tears began to sting her eyes. She replied, "I guess I just felt silly today." Hildy nudged Erika to hurry. Sydney slithered around the corner laughing.

12

The two friends planned to meet for breakfast at "The Vine" in the morning.

Hildy placed the new purchase in her hat closet.

As she lay in bed that night, the unkind words echoed in her mind. Tears streamed down her cheeks as she drifted off to sleep.

She awoke refreshed, ready to begin a new day. She brushed her teeth and skipped to the closet with excitement.

"My new hat will look perfect with my yellow sundress!"

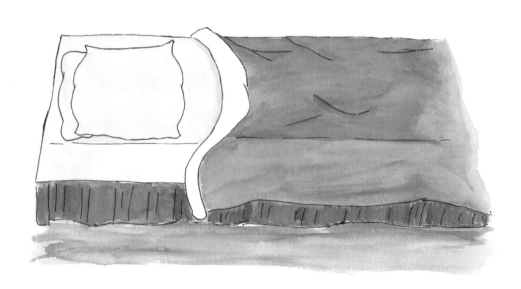

She opened the doors and gasped as she discovered the empty shelves upon which her fabulous collection was once displayed.

Hildy's stomach twisted into a knot.
She sank to the floor and began to cry.

Meanwhile, Erika waited at the café. Hildy was never late. She became worried and gulped down the last of her coffee.

19

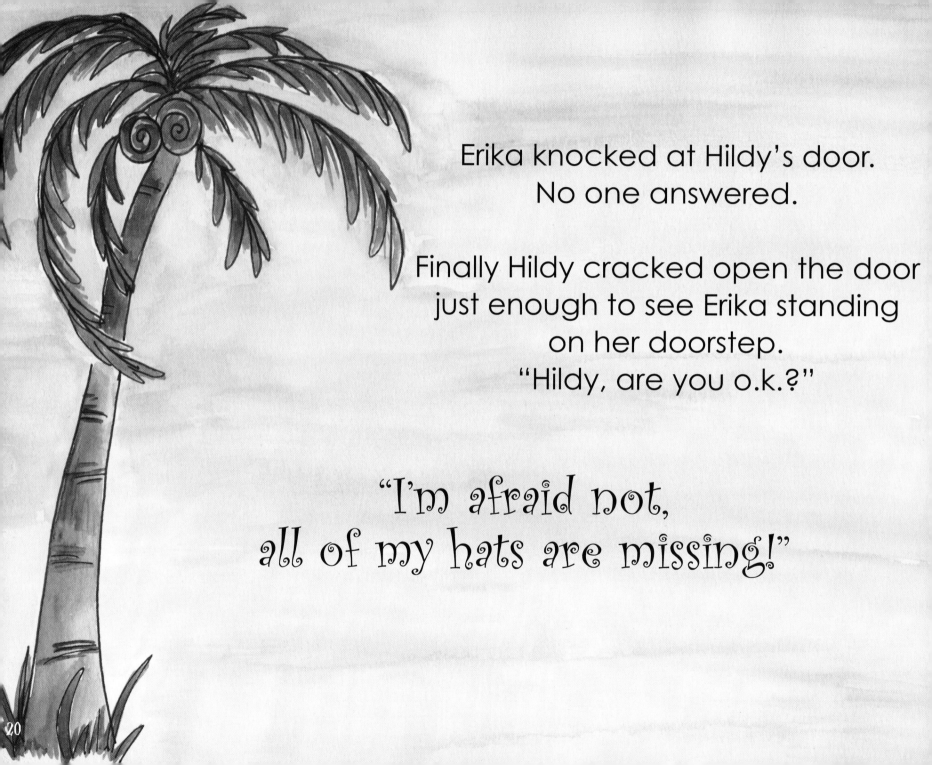

Erika knocked at Hildy's door.
No one answered.

Finally Hildy cracked open the door
just enough to see Erika standing
on her doorstep.
"Hildy, are you o.k.?"

"I'm afraid not,
all of my hats are missing!"

Erika knew how
devastated she must
be and offered to come
inside. Hildy reluctantly
opened the door.

21

"I am never leaving my house again," she cried.
"Well now, that's ridiculous!" answered Erika.
"There is no reason you can't leave this house!"

"Oh yes there is!" cried Hildy as she pulled off her night cap revealing her secret to her best friend. "I don't understand," said Erika. "What is the big deal?"

"I look ridiculous!"

said Hildy, "No one can see my crazy hair! They'll laugh!"

"So that's why you always wear hats?"

Hildy nodded. Erika reassured her,
"I think you're beautiful!"
Hildy looked up with a gleam of hope.

"Curls or no
curls,
hat or no hat,
I like you for you.
And so will your
other friends!"

23

"Maybe I don't need my hats after all," thought Hildy.

Erika said,
"Where's your dress?
Let's go show off
the *real* Hildy!"

Later, the village buzzed with excitement. Friends gathered around Hildy, but this time to admire her *natural curls.*

Sydney peered from a distance, confused. "Why is she still getting all that attention?"

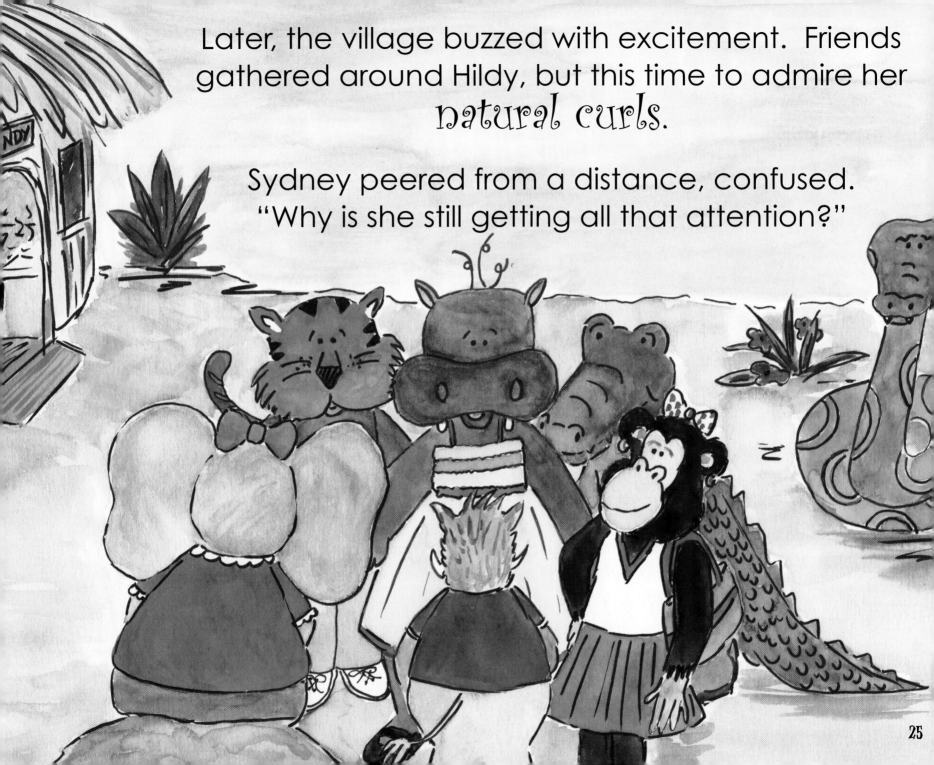

25

Hildy noticed the unusually sad look on Sydney's face.

"Is something wrong?"

Sydney answered, "I don't get it. Even without your cool hats, you have more friends than me!"

It all began to make sense. Hildy asked, "Did you take my hats?"

Sydney burst into tears and admitted, "Yesss, I am sooo sorry! I promise to give them back!"

"I forgive you," said Hildy with a big hug.

Sydney couldn't believe it. "But, I was so mean to you."

27

Hildy explained, "That's what friendship is all about. This actually helped me realize I just need to be myself. I don't have to hide under my hats anymore."

"What will you do with all your hats?"
asked Sydney.

Hildy thought for a moment. "I have an idea! Will you help me?"

Sydney and Hildy visited each of their friends that afternoon while Erika planned a party in Hildy's honor.
Everyone came wearing
one of Hildy's hats.
Everyone, that is,
except Hildy!

They all cheered,

"Hooray for Hildy!"

Author's Note

LeAnn lives with her husband and two sons in Nappanee, IN. She is an elementary school teacher with a passion for reading and writing. "Hooray For Hildy" is LeAnn's second children's book. The story was written specifically for the main character, Hildy, a hippo she has been doodling for years. LeAnn uses pen and watercolor to complete her cartoon illustrations.

"Hooray For Hildy" carries four strong messages inspired by the Bible: love, friendship, jealousy, and forgiveness. LeAnn feels strongly about teaching children good values and character. Visit her website to find Bible verses and discussion questions to share with your children. Use the verses to connect the story and their own lives.

LeAnn enjoyed visiting schools in 2005/2006. She was able to share the publishing journey of her first book, "When I Grow Up". She is available once again for school visits and plans to teach the children how to draw "Hildy". For more information, visit www.leannmiller.com.